"You stake

stories," Murlox angrily said.

"But even you cannot imagine the horrible things that I have seen in this world and the next. Flar cannot be defeated in this realm. It is not in our nature to seek the King."

He walked back over to Rainna. Murlox raised his staff over his head. The staff and his hands glowed with red energy. Lightning and thunder roared across the dark sky.

"The words of the Ancient Book are eternal!" Rainna cried out. "They cannot be destroyed! You need only to reach out your hand to the King to be saved!"

"Where is your King?" Murlox sarcastically said. "Why would He not save the Keeper of the Ancient Book? Your faith has failed you. Good-bye, princess."

Murlox placed his glowing red hand on her stomach. Rainna gasped. Her body was covered in a red haze. She struggled, her eyes and mouth wide open. She tried to speak, to scream, but she could not.

The Golden Knight #3
Rainna Falls

The Golden Knight #3
Rainna Falls

By
Steve Clark and **Justin Clark**

Based on Characters Created
By **Justin Clark**

Illustrations
By **Alison Fuller**

This is a work of fiction. All of the characters, organizations, and events portrayed in this story are either products of the authors' imaginations or are used fictitiously.

This book is being published in paperback and e-book format by New Horizons Press,
an imprint of That Guy Media, LLC
ISBN: 978-0-9647933-7-7

Published by New Horizons Press,
an imprint of That Guy Media, LLC.

New Horizons Press, an imprint of That Guy Media, LLC and associated logos are trademarks and/or registered trademarks of New Horizons Press, an imprint of That Guy Media, LLC.

Printed in the United States of America
10 9 8 7 6 5 4 3 2 1

I dedicate this book to my wife,
Leslie, and to our editor, Judy Faro.
For your support, encouragement and
help in making these books a reality.
-S.C.

To Alison Fuller,
for her amazing artwork.
-J.C.

And the Kingdom of the heavens and the evils of this world shall collide in battle....

And lo, the forces of Flar, the evil fire lord, shall make war upon the people who oppose him. He will bring his mighty armies to bear upon the ancient cities. The towers shall fall. The castle walls will tumble under his fiery fist. A mighty beast shall be called forth from the deepest pit and prowl the land. His arms shall be clawed and sharp. Fire shall shoot forth from his mouth. The sky shall darken so that not even the sun or moon may shine through it.

And in these times of tribulation, you,

1

the lost people, shall look for your King and your hearts will believe that he has abandoned you. But I say to you, the lost people, to look to the Kingdom for there is a ray of light. This ray of light can penetrate through any darkness. And then at that hour, the mighty armies of the King shall return to rescue you, his cherished people. His beloved archangel and his faithful soldiers of the light shall descend among you, his cherished people, and they shall be armed for battle, riding on white stallions and driving chariots of gold and silver.

The Prince shall fight the Evil One. Serpents shall strike at the Prince's sandaled feet, but they will do Him who is good and just no harm. The earth shall swallow the unjust. The Prince shall breathe new life into you, His cherished people, and renew your courage. The waters that He shall bring forth from the heavens shall wash your ways with righteous.

Oh, Rone, my precious city, why do you not heed my words that I give to you? Why must you turn away from your King?

Why have you forsaken the prophets that your King has sent to you for countless generations?

For once, you were a beautiful city and all the world looked to you in your splendor and envied your riches. Now, your city is empty. Your souls are hard and barren. Your people have turned away from you. The land no longer produces an abundance of crops.

But Rone, my precious city, even in your despair, in your wicked ways, you can still be restored. For you, His chosen people, shall see the righteousness and glory of the King descend from the Kingdom like a dove and renew His reign of peace and justice. You need only wait and make your watch ready for that time is drawing near. Where there is despair, my beloved people, in your hearts, your Prince shall give you hope. Where there is hate, my beloved people, in your minds, your Prince shall give you peace. For your King, my beloved people, is high above you and His ways are above your ways. From the wasteland and barren

3

desert, your King has led you forth and He will make for you a beautiful spring.

The wrongs of this generation and of the coming age shall be righted with the words and works of charity of the young. Do not fear their visions or ignore their voices. You, His chosen people, are one in the spirit with your King as the Prince is one in spirit with you. Be one, together, and bound by faith.

And behold, I saw the children of this generation gathered together in unity. And they worshiped their King together, holding in their hands a candle which shown out and its flame was eternal. The Golden Knight and the Keeper of the Great Book had been returned to the children of this generation.

And from within them, the Prince shall come forth and now dwells among us in the lands of our forefathers.

And so the prophecies have been told for countless generations....

5

Chapter One

The demon roared and pounded its clawed hands against its hairy chest. The creature opened its fanged mouth and a wave of fire shot out. The townspeople ran in terror to avoid being crushed by the monster's massive feet.

"W-w-we have a really big problem here," Franco stuttered out. "What is that thing?"

"It is a demon," the Golden Knight answered. "It has been summoned from the ancient pit."

"How do you plan on fighting something like that?" Franco questioned. "I hope that armor gives you some kind of special powers or something."

The Golden Knight drew his sword.

He placed his free hand on Franco's shoulder.

"This is not your battle to fight, Franco," he said. "Only my weapon can do it harm. Find safety with the others."

"You do not have to tell me twice," Franco replied. He gave a slight wave. "Good luck fighting that monster."

Franco turned and began to amble away. Suddenly, he stopped.

"No," Franco said, "I won't leave you."

"I cannot ask you to put yourself in danger," the Golden Knight remarked.

"Then do not ask," Franco replied. He began climbing further up the stone wall onto the next level of the parapet. "I may not be able to hurt that thing, but maybe I can distract it long enough for you to get a clear sword thrust at it. Just wait for my signal."

"And what signal shall you give?"

"Do not worry," Franco said with a smile. He bolted away. "You will know it when you see it."

"I have never liked signals such as that," the Golden Knight called out.

The demon trampled across the city. The Golden Knight climbed down the castle wall to the street. He carefully followed. Suddenly, the monster turned and threw a ball of fire at him.

"Shield," the Golden Knight commanded. A golden shield materialized in his left hand. The fire ball struck the shield and vanished in a cloud of smoke. The demon continued. The Golden Knight began to follow again. Passing one of the burning houses, he heard a child's cry coming from inside. The Golden Knight entered the doorway.

"Is there someone inside?" he called out through the smoke.

There was a cough from the far corner. The Golden Knight walked through the haze toward the sound. Fire surrounded him, but he felt no heat. There, huddled in the corner, a small, ten-year old boy sat. He had no shoes and his clothes were ragged. There was a wooden cage beside him. Inside the cage, there was a rabbit chewing on grass.

"You must leave and take refuge outside," the Golden Knight said. "It is not safe for you to be here."

"I cannot leave my rabbit," the boy replied, "and I cannot get the cage to open."

"You would give your very life for this rabbit?" the Golden Knight asked. "He must be a special rabbit then. We

11

shall save him too."

The Golden Knight struck the cage with his sword. It collapsed into pieces. The boy grabbed the rabbit and cradled it in his arms. He tucked it underneath his shirt. The fire was engulfing the house in flames.

"We're trapped!" the boy cried out. "We are going to burn!"

The Golden Knight placed his sword in its sheath. He stretched out his armored hands. The wall of fire parted. There was a clear, dirt path now leading out of the house. The Golden Knight and the boy walked harmlessly between the flames and escaped to safety.

"Find your father and mother," the Golden Knight said.

"Who has sent you," the boy gasped, "that you can do such powerful things?"

"The King," the Golden Knight

12

replied. "The creator of all the universe."

"It's a she," the boy said. "My rabbit, I mean. It is a girl. I think she is going to have a bunch of baby rabbits soon."

The boy turned and ran away. The Golden Knight smiled.

Franco crept along the high castle wall. He had managed to get behind the demon. He looked down at the short sword that Demetrius had given him.

"This is not going to help much against that thing," he said. He put the sword on his belt. "So it is time to make a little noise."

Franco raced in front of the demon. He waved his hands wildly and shouted. The monster turned.

"All right," Franco said to himself. "Something should be happening about now. And this is not it."

The demon swung his clawed hand

13

and swatted Franco off the castle wall like a house fly. Franco flew through the air, screaming and tumbling as he went. He crashed into a farmer's cart filled with piles of straw. The Golden Knight raced over to him.

"Are you all right?" the Golden Knight asked, digging Franco out from the pile of straw in the cart.

Franco brushed the straw and dirt from his hair and face. He blew out pieces of straw from his mouth.

"Did you not see the signal?" he gasped. Franco sat up in the cart.

"What signal did you provide?" the Golden Knight asked.

"This signal," Franco shot back. He waved his arms frantically over his head. "You know, the signal."

"I did not see it. I was preoccupied

with another matter," the Golden Knight replied. "Are you sure no bones are broken?"

Franco rose to his feet with a slight groan and jumped down from the cart. "I'm not going to ask. You were probably saving some bunny rabbit or something. But do not worry, I will survive," he remarked. "I have been thrown off more castle walls than just that one."

"Actually... you have been fortunate," the Golden Knight said. "When I was a young boy, I played a game where a ball was kicked between two markings on the side of the barn. One day, I was...."

"Not the best time to tell me about life on the farm," Franco sarcastically replied. "You know, we have a monster walking around destroying the city."

The demon had trampled his way over to the north wall of Rone.

"Now is our chance," Franco noted. "I will distract it and you do whatever it is that you need to do."

"Are you sure that you wish to attempt this action again?" the Golden Knight asked.

"Just remember," Franco said, waving his hands over his head. "This is the signal."

Franco darted off toward the castle wall. He began climbing a ladder to the top.

"It leads us further and further away from the cathedral," the Golden Knight pondered. "Further away from Princess Rainna and the Ancient Book."

17

Chapter Two

Marsonee, the mighty archangel, and Flar, the evil fire lord, squared off against one another in the skies over the ancient city of Rone. Dark clouds were beginning to form. Flaming boulders, fired from the fire army's catapults outside the city, whistled past them. Flar and Marsonee exchanged sword blows, each darting about the sky on their powerful wings.

"You have started this final war which will destroy these ruined people," Flar roared, his flaming sword locking against Marsonee's blade.

"There is a peace which may only come after war," Marsonee replied, "a lasting, eternal peace which will endure."

"I have given these people security," Flar said. "I have freed them from the oppression of the King."

"At what price is your security?" Marsonee retorted. "You have taken their freedom. You have taken their free will."

"Your promise of free will is only an illusion," the fire lord replied. "These people are incapable of ruling themselves."

Their blades locked with an explosion of electricity.

"Even when they were given paradise," Flar continued, "how quickly and easily they turned away from their King. Time and time again throughout the ages, He has tried to gather the wayward ones onto Himself. Theirs is a history of sin and failure."

"You tricked them with lies and

deceit," Marsonee replied.

"They will betray you again," the fire lord said. His eyes glowed a fiery red. "You know in your heart it will be true. The Golden Knight cannot save them. The Keeper cannot save them. Neither can you."

Marsonee hesitated and slowly backed away.

"You doubt the prophecy, too," Flar confidently remarked. "You always have doubted the worthiness of these pathetic people ever since the Great Divide was formed. I can give you true power and kingdoms to rule. Turn your back on them before they betray you once again."

The archangel covered his one ear with his free hand as he tried to block out Flar's words. Marsonee shook his head in defiance.

"No! Never shall I fail my King!" Marsonee cried out. He rushed forward locking blades once again with the evil fire lord.

~

The King stood on the castle walls staring out at the Great Divide. Near the boundary of the supernatural energy field, thousands of angels had gathered, hovering in winged formation. The Prince approached the King.

"Beshtar and the angels are ready, my King," he said. "They await your command."

The King rubbed his white beard. "Long have the people of the physical realm suffered," the King said. "I have heard the cries of the oppressed, of the widow and the orphaned. And as I freed them from slavery and exile generations ago and brought their forefathers from the desert forth into the promised kingdom, I shall do so again if only they would call on my name. As they have forsaken my prophecies, have they forgotten me, my son?"

"Not forgotten you, my King," the Prince replied. "You have been hidden from their sight. The words of the Ancient Book have been twisted and distorted to serve an evil aim. They wait only for a brighter way to be revealed to them once again."

"Those who wait upon their King shall renew their strength and they shall mount up with wings as eagles," the King remarked. "I will give them strength so they will not grow weary when they run. I shall make it so they shall not faint in the sweltering heat."

They began to walk down the castle ramparts.

"They are a hard and stubborn people," the Prince said. "Even when I myself walked among them, despite all they had heard and the miracles they had seen, so many could still not believe. But there is courage and love in their hearts. It remains."

"They are made in our very image," the King replied, "and we have breathed the spirit of life in their bosoms. But they have become trapped by the complexities of the fruit of which they taste. They have forgotten the nature of their spiritual being. All creation can be redeemed. I have never lost faith in that."

"Shall I command Beshtar to take his army through the Great Divide?" the Prince questioned. "Marsonee and the Golden Knight cannot defeat Flar and his evil alone."

"No," the King answered. "It will be the young that will save the old of this generation. When they call on us, only then shall we come to their aid."

Flar raised his spiked, armored

hand.

"Marsonee, let us see how well you deal with fire," Flar roared. Flames shot out of Flar's hand.

Marsonee stretched out his arm. A wall of sparkling water formed in front of him. The dark fire slammed into the water. Immediately, the fire evaporated into steam. Flar blasted away at Marsonee's defense to no avail. Frustrated by his inability to break the wall of water, Flar stopped his fiery assault. The sparkling water disappeared.

"Your evil ways cannot compare to the greatness of the King," the archangel said.

Flar surged forward and locked blades with Marsonee. The fire lord was still strong and powerful. Marsonee grimaced with determination to keep Flar from pushing him back. Sweat began to form on the archangel's forehead.

"Do you tire, Marsonee?" Flar taunted. "I am not bound by the limitations of this realm as you are."

"I shall not tire," Marsonee remarked through clenched teeth, "so long as you exist in this world."

"You have more to worry about than just me," Flar replied.

Suddenly, there was a flaming boulder rocketing toward Marsonee. The archangel pushed Flar away. Marsonee turned and with one powerful stroke, struck the rock with his sword. It split into two pieces. Flar knew this was his opportunity. With a gust of his wings, the fire lord flew forward and swung his flaming sword. Marsonee pivoted back to avoid the blow. However, he was not fast enough. Flar's blade clipped the bottom of Marsonee's right wing, setting the feathers on fire.

"Argh!"Marsonee cried out in pain. He struggled to remain airborne, but with every flap of his wings, the fire only grew. Marsonee knew he would have to land or risk his entire wing being engulfed in flame. Marsonee spiraled downward, a trail of smoke in his wake. He hit the ground hard, dropping his sword and rolling several feet in the dirt. As the archangel rolled, the fire on his wing was slowly extinguished. Marsonee struggled to stand but could not. Flar landed several feet away. His demonic wings folded up on his armored back. Flar began walking toward the wounded archangel.

"You are weak," Flar admonished. "You are but a shell of your former self."

Marsonee struggled to crawl toward his sword. With inches to go, he reached out for it. Flar kicked it away

with his boot.

"Your time is at an end," Flar said.

"Even if you destroy me," Marsonee replied. "There will be others."

"No," Flar retorted. "They have resigned themselves to their fate behind the Great Divide."

Flar raised his flaming sword high over his towering head. With one powerful stroke, the fire lord swung it down toward Marsonee's head.

Chapter Three

Princess Rainna rested unconscious on the marble floor of the cathedral. Adjusting his robes, Murlox knelt down and stroked her long, dark hair. His body transformed into an ugly, old man.

"Sleep well, my dear princess," he said. "Your time is passing and soon you will be nothing more than a distant memory."

Murlox looked over at the Ancient Book resting beside her.

"Why do you not protect her from my evil? Why would you allow her to suffer in this way?" the sorcerer questioned. "Perhaps you have some other grand design that this world cannot know."

Murlox stood and gazed around the weathered cathedral.

"I remember this place from another time so long ago," he whispered in sadness. His voice still managed to echo throughout the empty sanctuary. "Back when my faith was as strong as hers. Now you have abandoned her just as once you did me."

The old Murlox walked over to the broken stone altar. He ran his wrinkled hand across the table. Through the shattered stained glass windows, Murlox could hear the fire boulders smashing against the ground and the sounds of screaming and chaos.

"They once found a peace here," he said. "Those sad, pathetic people running around like chickens out there. But then, you would no longer hear them. You ceased to listen. It was almost as if you had disappeared. What was I to say to them when they were to come here to me? Flar's promises were real to them. They were real to me."

Murlox saw the long spiral staircase located in the corner of the church which led up to the former bell tower. His crooked face smiled.

"There is no power here," he cackled. "Only my dark magic remains. I must prepare the sacrifice as the Lord Flar has commanded me."

He turned back to the altar and raised his staff. The staff glowed with dark energy which soon engulfed the broken table. In seconds, the two broken segments of the stone altar rejoined together and vanished. Rainna slowly began to stir with a slight moan. She sat up and balanced herself with one arm while placing her other hand on the side of her face. Murlox quickly returned to his youthful appearance.

"Murlox?" she said, still dazed and confused. "What are you...?"

"Do not try to escape me, princess," the sorcerer said. He pointed his staff at her. Magical ropes formed and tied around her hands. "We have quite a climb to make together."

"I will not go with you," Rainna said. She struggled to sit completely upright. Rainna turned to see the Book lying near her. "The ancient Law will protect me."

"Will it now?" Murlox boasted.

The Book was suddenly engulfed in a white light and disappeared.

"No," Rainna gasped in disbelief.

"You have no choice in this matter, my little girl," Murlox said as he calmly walked down from the altar area. Despite her resistance, Murlox pulled Rainna to her feet. "All is now in place. The final act of this drama is set to begin."

34

The sorcerer dragged Princess Rainna over to the staircase.

"Your evil will not prevail here!" she cried out.

"Climb," Murlox commanded. He pushed her with his staff onto the first step.

"What lies at the top of the tower?" Rainna questioned.

"Your destiny, of course," Murlox grimaced. He pushed her in the back again.

Reluctantly, Rainna started up the wooden stairs.

~

Demetrius, the crazy, old priest, raced down the narrow streets of Rone. All around him, frightened townspeople were running in panic, dodging flaming fire boulders and trying to find shelter for their children. Demetrius spied a large wooden wagon filled with straw resting against a stone wall. A large crowd had gathered around it. A couple of men were trying to harness horses to the wagon. Demetrius bolted up the wheel and climbed into the wagon. The horses galloped off.

"People of Rone, hear me!" the old priest cried out.

The townspeople ignored him and continued rushing about the square and down the dirty streets.

"People of Rone listen! I beg of you to hear me!" Demetrius called out again. "Your King has delivered you!"

At these words, several members of the crowd stopped to listen. Everyone, including the children, began to gather around the wagon where Demetrius stood.

"Delivered us, you say?" a ragged man shockingly questioned. "He has done no such thing! He has brought fire

down from the sky and a demon to our gates! How has our King delivered us?"

"We must plead for mercy from Lord Flar!" a woman, her face caked with dirt, begged to the others. She held a baby in her arms. A little girl, wearing a torn blanket for clothes, stood beside her. "For the sake of our children, we must!"

The other townspeople grumbled their approval and nodded their heads. Demetrius, moved with pity for their ignorance, jumped down from the wagon and approached the little girl. He embraced her.

"And what mercy, I ask of all of you, can you expect to receive from the fire lord?" Demetrius asked. "I ask all of you, what mercy has he brought to you thus far? Your toil and labor, he requires of you. Your harvest, he takes from you.

Your homes, he destroys. Your city is now besieged."

The townspeople once again grumbled in approval. They knew that what the old priest spoke was true.

"Look at yourselves," Demetrius continued. "Why is it that you choose not to see? Would you trade the souls of your children to the great deceiver? And for what? The Golden Knight has returned to you. The Ancient Book of the Law, the very words of the Prince, has been opened for you. What other signs do you require before you will begin to believe again?"

"What would you expect us to do, Demetrius?" an old man sighed. He wore a dusted, formal garment. "As you know, I was once one of the constables in Rone. These are nothing but a small and helpless people."

"What I ask is simple," Demetrius

replied. He walked to the center of the crowd and placed his arms on the constable's shoulders. "Open your hearts again for they have been hardened. Believe in your King. Long have you suffered. Long have you waited. The time for your freedom is now."

"Show us!" a man called out. "Show us the power of our King!"

"Look then! Look to the skies, you who are faint of heart," the old priest retorted. Demetrius pointed upward. "The King has sent his mighty archangel to fight for you."

The townspeople gazed skyward. They could see Marsonee and Flar battling and trading sword blows. The crowd gasped in amazement at the sight. Suddenly, Flar's sword struck Marsonee's wing. Marsonee spiraled to the ground, a trail of smoke behind him. Demetrius buried his head in his hands.

The townspeople pointed in horror and fell silent.

"Run! Run for your lives! Save yourselves!" the constable suddenly cried out.

"Wait! Wait! We can look someplace else!" Demetrius pleaded. "The Golden Knight..."

The Golden Knight and Franco somersaulted through the air with a prolonged shout and crashed through the straw roof of one of the nearby houses. In the distance, the demon roared in delight. They stumbled out of the house. The Golden Knight immediately started back up the street. Demetrius raced over to Franco, who was holding his head and leaning against the door. The crowd followed.

"How goes it, my young friend?" the priest asked. "Are you hurt?"

"This is starting to remind me of

that time I wrestled bears in the traveling circus," Franco remarked. "But do not worry, preacher, I think we got that thing distracted now. I can tell he is getting tired from throwing half the city around. We got this."

"Tell me, my son," Demetrius whispered into Franco's ear, "did you ever manage to beat one of those big furry bears?"

Suddenly, a flaming house flew over their heads and crashed into the ground several hundred feet away. The demon roared. The townspeople bolted in panic.

"Not a great time for me to answer that question," Franco remarked. He started back up the street. Franco turned back to the old priest. "But do not worry. I am telling you. We got this."

Demetrius looked around and saw that the townspeople had dispersed and melted away. All that remained was a little ten-year-old boy with no shoes, ragged clothes, and a dirty face.

"I must take some time and work on my sermons," the old priest sighed. "Are you all that remains?"

"I will fight for you," the young boy sheepishly said, "and for the King."

Demetrius smiled and hobbled over to the boy. He knelt down and touched his cheek.

"If only your elders held just a portion of your faith, my child," Demetrius remarked. "What mountains they would have moved. Come. Let me get you to safety."

The priest led the child around a corner. A mother let out a gasp and raced out from one of the houses. She scooped the little boy up in her arms and embraced him.

"Thank you, father," she said as

tears began to form in her eyes. "We thought we had lost him."

From the houses and out of the alleys, the men of Rone began to appear again. They walked out into the streets carrying pitchforks and wooden clubs. A handful of the men carried swords and primitive shields. A few wore chain mail armor. They were led by the old constable.

"We are not cowards. We will fight for our families and for this city," the constable said. "We will fight for our King. We ask only that you lead the way."

Demetrius smiled and rolled up his sleeves. "Follow me then," he replied.

~

Murlox pushed open the bell tower door with his staff and shoved Rainna outside onto the platform. The cathedral ramparts towered hundreds of feet over the city. Rainna could see the demon smashing through Rone, fire shooting from its hideous mouth. She watched the flaming boulders raining down from the sky onto the helpless people below. She saw the Golden Knight.

"What has Flar done?" she gasped.

"You are witnessing the fate of all those who would oppose the Lord Flar. It is Armageddon for this place," Murlox replied. "But do not worry for them, princess. For you shall not survive to see their destruction."

Overhead, dark clouds began to form and swirl. Lightning crackled across the sky. Thunder crashed. On the tower platform, the stone altar, originally in the church sanctuary, suddenly materialized before Murlox and Rainna.

"Lie down on it," the sorcerer commanded.

"No," Rainna replied. "I will not."

45

"You are defiant even until the very end," Murlox said. "Be it as you wish, princess."

Murlox twirled his fingers before Rainna's face. She let out a gasp as her green eyes glazed over white. Princess Rainna slumped into Murlox's arms.

"You have no power without the Ancient Book," the sorcerer grinned. He placed her on the altar. Murlox slowly transformed back into his older, uglier form. Carefully, the old sorcerer tied her hands and feet to the stone table. "You have no purpose, my sweet Rainna."

Murlox slowly hobbled over to the edge of the tower ramparts. He could see Flar's mighty army displayed on the plains outside of the city.

"My magic would not have her sleep long," he whispered. "Once she has awakened, I shall be able to begin."

Murlox turned back toward Rainna.

46

Suddenly, there was a flash of white light which temporarily blinded him. As his vision returned, the old sorcerer could see the Ancient Book had appeared and was lying next to the sleeping princess.

Chapter Four

Franco cautiously crept unnoticed across the castle wall. The demon roared in front of him, beating its chest. Franco crouched down behind a pile of rocks.

"Now how do I get that things attention?" Franco whispered under his breath. He looked around the ramparts and noticed some square stones lying nearby. "Look at that. Those will do nicely."

Franco crawled over to the stones and gathered them. He shuffled along the wall and was able to get close to the back of the demon. He slowly rose and began throwing the square stones. They bounced harmlessly off the monster's hairy back.

"Hey, ugly!" Franco yelled out.

"Look over here, you monster!"

The demon turned with a roar.

"Now! Now!" Franco yelled, frantically waving his arms over his head. He looked down from the castle wall. Franco did not see the Golden Knight anywhere. He lowered his arms. "Oh no, not this again."

The demon roared and pounded its fists against its chest again. Its mouth began to glow with a fiery red mist.

"Oh, no. No, no, no!" Franco shouted. He took off running down the castle parapet. A ball of fire shot from the demon's mouth, exploding just feet away from Franco. Tiny pieces of flame and stone showered down on him.

"This is not good," he muttered. "Not good at all."

Franco started running. The demon's clawed hand crashed into the castle wall. The wall shook and began to crack under Franco's feet.

"This is going to hurt," Franco whispered.

The wall collapsed, sending Franco plummeting to the ground in a cloud of dust and stone. He painfully crawled out of the rubble and debris, propping himself up against a large rock. Franco rubbed his head and tried to collect his senses. A large shadow fell over him. Franco slowly looked up. The demon reached down with its clawed hand and wrapped it around him. It raised Franco off the ground and let out a roar. The demon opened its mouth. There were sharp fangs and fire.

"I think this thing is really going to try to eat me," Franco observed as he struggled against its iron grip. "I could use a little help here."

Franco glanced around, looking for any way he might escape. Marsonee fell from the sky in a trail of smoke. He crashed to the ground, landing out of sight from Franco. Flar slowly descended behind him. Franco gasped.

"I do not think this is going exactly as we planned," he said. "And I was just starting to believe..."

Suddenly, three golden arrows flew through the air and struck the demon's arm. The monster cried out in pain. Franco looked down. There on the ground, the Golden Knight stood. The Golden Knight raised his bow. The weapon was shiny gold and could hold three arrows at one time. He fired. The arrows hit the demon's hand. The monster dropped Franco. He fell with a shout.

"Wings," the Golden Knight commanded as the bow disappeared. There was a sparkling of the air behind the Golden Knight. A pair of white,

angelic wings materialized on his back. He rose off the ground and quickly accelerated. The Golden Knight grabbed the falling Franco.

"A bow and arrows? Wings," Franco exclaimed. "Where are you getting these things?"

"I ask the King for them," the Golden Knight replied. "And He strengthens me so that I may do His will."

They circled around the demon and landed behind the creature. The Golden Knight drew his sword. The demon clutched its wounded hand.

"It is confused. You hurt it," Franco observed. "Now may be our chance."

The Golden Knight rocketed up into the sky. As the demon turned, the Golden Knight embedded his sword into the monster's chest with one thrust. The demon let loose a demonic roar and collapsed to the ground in a cloud of dust and smoke. The body burst into flames and disintegrated into a pile of black ash. A gust of wind blew the ashes away.

"Now that is not very fair," Franco remarked. "I was planning to get that thing mounted on my wall."

"We must move quickly," the Golden Knight said. He placed his sword in its sheath. "I fear our fighting this demon has only been a diversion for Murlox's true mission."

"Wait. Who is Murlox?" Franco gasped. "A diversion? For what? No offense, chief, but I thought fighting that thing was awful hard."

"There is little time to explain," the Golden Knight replied. "Murlox is a dark sorcerer. He had the demon lead us away from the cathedral so Princess Rainna and the Ancient Book would be

left unprotected. He seeks to destroy the princess. We must get there to help her."

"How come I do not know any of these things?" Franco exclaimed, throwing his hands in the air.

"Another signal?" the Golden Knight said.

"So now you get it," Franco said with a smile.

"Let us get to the cathedral."

Franco grabbed the Golden Knight's arm.

"Marsonee was wounded," Franco said. "I saw him fall from the sky. I think he landed not far from the town square. Flar was right behind him."

"He is my friend," the Golden Knight said. "I cannot leave him. But the Keeper must be defended at all costs."

"The Keeper? I thought we were talking about Princess Rainna?" Franco remarked.

"We are."

"Let me protect the princess," Franco insisted. "I will find that crazy, old priest, Demetrius, to help me."

The Golden Knight thought for a moment.

"You have no weapon," he said.

"Do not worry," Franco said. He turned and started to run down the street. "I will make do. I am very resourceful."

"Yes," the Golden Knight whispered. "You certainly are."

~

Flar raised his flaming fire sword over his massive armored body. Marsonee struggled to his knees.

"Beg for my mercy," the fire lord commanded.

"In you, there is no mercy," Marsonee replied.

"So be it then," Flar growled. He

swung his fire sword down toward Marsonee's head.

Without warning, the Golden Knight raced into the courtyard, drew his sword and deflected the fire lord's blade away.

"What?" Flar roared.

"Stand back," the Golden Knight said firmly.

"How dare you try to command me," Flar hissed. "You have no power over me."

The Golden Knight raised his armored hand. A powerful gust of wind struck Flar in the chest and threw him across the square into a stone wall. Rocks toppled down onto the fire lord.

"That should give us enough time to get you to safety," the Golden Knight said.

"Your timing is impeccable, boy," Marsonee commented. "But do not be

concerned for me."

The Golden Knight helped Marsonee to his feet. He reached down and collected the archangel's sword.

"I am concerned for all my friends," the Golden Knight said. He handed Marsonee his weapon.

"There is still much fight in me," the archangel replied.

"I shall fight Flar," the Golden Knight said.

"There is a storm overhead," Marsonee remarked, noting the dark twirling clouds over Rone. "They are centered on the ancient cathedral. Princess Rainna, is she the one?"

"Franco and Demetrius shall see that she and the Ancient Book are safe."

The Golden Knight guided Marsonee to one of the villager's houses. Three women ran out of the door and helped the archangel inside. He sat down on a straw bed.

"He is injured," the Golden Knight said. "Please care for him."

"We shall," one of the women replied. "If it be needed."

They immediately began to tend to the archangel's wound and wipe his forehead of dirt.

The Golden Knight took a final look at his angelic friend before he exited the house. Marsonee gently brushed the three women aside.

"Your kindness is welcomed but unnecessary," Marsonee said, rising to his feet. "Where are the men of Rone? I wish to lead them in battle."

The three women smiled.

Chapter Five

Franco darted across the town square toward the cathedral. Looking up, he saw the dark clouds twirling like a cyclone above the highest tower on the ancient church. Lightning bolts flashed out. Then Franco saw the large flaming stone pierce through the clouds and descend directly at him. He rolled to his right, barely avoiding the burning rock as it impacted into the ground. Franco rose to his feet and brushed off the dirt.

"I do not know what is worse," he muttered to himself, "that monster or the flying rocks."

Demetrius was directing the women and children as they rushed to find shelter. The men of Rone were grabbing pitchforks and organizing on the far side of the square. Franco saw the old priest and motioned to him.

"Demetrius!" Franco called out. "I need your help! We have to save Princess Rainna from the sorcerer!"

"Where is she?" the priest said.

"Up there," Franco responded, pointing to the high tower on the cathedral. "The Golden Knight said that the sorcerer would try to destroy the Ancient Book. He said that Rainna was the key."

"Murlox is powerful," Demetrius responded. "He will not be defeated easily."

They arrived at the cathedral steps. Franco noticed the horses still tied to the posts outside the main entrance, and he tossed the short sword to Demetrius.

"You are going to need this old man," he said as he walked over to the horses.

"And what of you, Franco?" Demetrius asked. "We stand little chance if you have no weapon."

Franco began rummaging through Rainna's saddlebag. He pulled out the fire sword and activated the flaming blade. He cut the ropes holding the horses. Twirling the sword above his head, Franco rushed the horses away to safety.

"This sword should do just fine," Franco remarked. "Let us go."

Franco and Demetrius entered the cathedral. Despite all the chaos outside, the sanctuary was quiet, almost peaceful.

"How did you remember the fire sword was there?" Demetrius asked.

"I was a thief," Franco answered. "You learn how to notice and remember things. How do we get up to that tower?"

"There is a staircase. Come quickly, this way," the old priest said as they raced off. "I fear we have little time."

"Let me go!" Rainna screamed. She struggled vainly against the chains holding her hands and feet. "Who are you? You will never succeed with terror and fear!"

The old sorcerer hobbled across the tower platform and leaned over her. He stroked her hair and ran his bony fingers down her arm.

"Do not touch me!" she said, struggling to move away.

"You are the key, my dear princess," Murlox said. "But you are not the door. Does my face frighten you? Does it remind you of a time from long ago?"

"I do not know you!" Rainna called back.

"No," Murlox replied. "I imagine in this form that you do not."

He stumbled over to the Book.

65

"You stake your hope on ancient stories," Murlox angrily said. "But even you cannot imagine the horrible things that I have seen in this world and the next. Flar cannot be defeated in this realm. It is not in our nature to seek the King."

He walked back over to Rainna. Murlox raised his staff over his head. The staff and his hands glowed with red energy. Lightning and thunder roared across the dark sky.

"The words of the Ancient Book are eternal!" Rainna cried out. "They cannot be destroyed! You need only to reach out your hand to the King to be saved!"

"Where is your King?" Murlox sarcastically said. "Why would He not save the Keeper of the Ancient Book? Your faith has failed you. Good-bye, princess."

Murlox placed his glowing red

hand on her stomach. Rainna gasped. Her body was covered in a red haze. She struggled, her eyes and mouth wide open. She tried to speak, to scream, but she could not.

"Do not resist," Murlox said. "Feel your life force leaving you."

Rainna slowly turned her head and gazed at the Book. It sat motionless. A tear fell from her face. She gasped again and closed her eyes. Her body went limp. The red haze disappeared. Murlox removed his hand from her stomach.

Demetrius and Franco burst through the wooden door leading out of the tower. Murlox turned to face them.

"Step away from the girl, Murlox," Demetrius forcefully said.

"Demetrius, I should have known you would still be alive after all this time," Murlox groaned. "You are too late. Princess Rainna is already gone. She has fallen into the eternal sleep."

"If that is true," Franco angrily said. "You are going to pay for that, old man."

"Be wise, my young friend," Demetrius whispered. "Do not let his outer appearance fool you. Murlox is a powerful warrior regardless of the form he chooses to take."

"You have failed, Demetrius," Murlox said. "Your city is being destroyed. The Book now belongs to me."

"It shall serve you no purpose," the priest replied. "You cannot open it."

"But neither can you or your companions," Murlox retorted. "And that is what matters the most, is it not? You cannot have faith without its foundations."

"I have had enough of your talk, you crazy wizard," Franco said. "I am taking back the Book and Princess Rainna."

"Come and take them," the sorcerer said. Murlox slowly began transforming into his younger bodily form. Franco gasped in amazement. "Surely you do not fear an old man such as I. Come, if you dare my young fool."

Franco lunged forward with the flaming sword. He threw several quick blows, but Murlox easily deflected them with his staff. Murlox jumped back, twirling the staff over his head. Franco threw more thrusts, but once again Murlox brushed them aside.

"Do you really think that you are a match for me, boy?" Murlox remarked. "I have walked every battlefield on this world for a thousand years."

Murlox pointed his staff at Franco. A beam of energy shot out. Franco raised his sword. The energy beam struck the

flaming blade, throwing Franco across the tower platform. Franco quickly rose to his feet.

"Lightning, consume him!" Murlox roared.

Bolts of lightning rocketed down from the sky. Franco dove and rolled across the stone flooring as the electrical blasts exploded around him.

"You are quick," Murlox observed, "but are you faster than the wind itself?"

Murlox threw up his arms. A powerful gust of wind surged forward hitting Franco.in the chest. Franco fell backwards, dropping his fire sword. He toppled over the stone ramparts.

"Franco!" Demetrius called out.

Franco hung from the tower wall. He struggled to maintain his grip. Murlox walked over to the edge and looked down at him. Franco glanced down at the ground below him.

"This is not good," he muttered.

"You are strong," Murlox remarked, tapping his staff next to Franco's hand. "Your heart has not been corrupted. A worthy adversary you might have been. Enjoy the fall."

Demetrius bolted through the air with a yell. Murlox turned and deflected the priest's sword thrust. They exchanged several blows as they moved across the tower surface. Demetrius moved quickly, leaping and tumbling as he threw sword thrusts. Murlox was equally fast, turning and blocking as he went.

"Time has not failed your fighting skills," Murlox said, "but warrior priests are a relic from another age. The great crusades are over for this world. Men have chosen their own foolish way."

Murlox pointed his bandaged hand at Demetrius. A blast of energy shot out and hit the old priest. Demetrius cried out in pain, dropping his short sword. He stumbled backwards and fell beside the stone altar where Rainna's body lay.

"Look at her, Demetrius," Murlox grinned. The sorcerer bent down and picked up the short sword lying on the ground. With the sword in his left hand and his staff in his right hand, he pressed the edge of the blade against the old priest's chest. "She was so young and naïve. What has her faith given her?"

"There is a power that you could never understand," Demetrius stammered out. "And this power will ultimately save her from your darkness."

"Will it save you, too?" Murlox laughed.

Franco braced his legs against the stone tower and pulled himself back over the stone wall. He crawled forward, grabbed the fire sword, and rose to his feet.

"Murlox!" he cried out. Lightning crashed over his head.

The surprised sorcerer turned at the sound of Franco's voice. Franco hurled the fire sword through the air with one easy motion. The flaming blade sliced through Murlox's bandaged left hand. Murlox screamed in pain and stumbled back. Patches of dust fell from the wound in Murlox's hand.

"What have you done to me?" Murlox gasped. "I cannot be defeated! I have destroyed the Keeper of the Ancient Book!"

Suddenly, the Book was bathed in light from a sun beam which had penetrated the twirling dark clouds. The stones underneath Murlox's feet started to shake and rumble. Murlox stumbled back as he lost his footing. A bolt of lightning shot down from the sky and

75

struck him.

"No!" he cried out. Murlox slowly began changing back to his older form. "What is happening? I control the forces of nature in this realm!"

A second blast of lightning and then a third bolt hit him. His robes were smoking. A powerful gust of wind rushed across the tower. Murlox reached out, but there was nothing for him to hold. He fell backwards with a yell and disappeared over the tower ramparts. Demetrius and Franco ran to the edge. They peered over the walls but could see nothing.

"We won," Demetrius muttered out. "We defeated the sorcerer."

Franco turned away and saw Rainna's body lying on the altar.

"Did we?" he asked.

Chapter Six

Murlox, shaped as a young man, hobbled through the barren fields outside of Rone. The evil sorcerer still clutched the bandaged stump where his hand had once been before his battle with Franco and Demetrius on the cathedral tower. Grey dust trickled out between his clinched fingers. Outside the city of Rone, Flar's mighty fire army stood in formation firing catapults of flaming boulders into the town. The flags of Lord Flar flapped in the wind. Murlox made his way over to the fire soldier commander. A black armored stallion uneasily rested nearby. Murlox struggled as he slowly mounted the war horse. The horse, its red eyes glowing, snorted

black clouds of smoke as it adjusted to the weight of its new rider.

"You may cease your bombardment of the city at once," Murlox commanded.

The fire soldier commander turned to his troops. He raised his armored hand. The fire soldiers manning the catapults immediately stopped loading their weapons.

"Move your infantry forward and take the city," Murlox instructed. "The townspeople are trying to organize a resistance. Destroy them all."

The fire soldier commander nodded. He raised his flaming sword. Seconds passed. The fire soldier commander lowered his sword in a swift movement. Several fire soldiers, using long bones as drumsticks, began to beat their red drums in a slow, monotone cadence. The fire infantry drew their swords in unison and activated the flaming blades. They raised their shields and let out a strong, demonic shout. The infantry divisions of Flar's fire army moved silently forward in six rows of six columns with six fire soldiers in each.

"Concentrate your assault on the main gate," Murlox ordered. "When you have secured the perimeters of the city, massacre the main body of natives that are forming in the town square. Lord Flar will not tolerate defeat. There is only victory."

The fire soldier commander nodded. The sorcerer pulled the reins on the horse's harness and galloped away.

"Away from me, you annoying stone!" Flar roared as he burst free from the pile of rocks. He brushed his dark armor off with a swipe of his massive arms. "Surely, you did not believe such a simple trick of the wind could stop one such as I."

"End your attack, fire lord," the Golden Knight said. "You have done enough damage to these innocent people and their homes."

"No. I will not cease," Flar replied. Balls of fire formed in his fists. "I will see you surrender to me first!"

Flar threw the fire balls with fury. The Golden Knight deflected and chopped them to pieces with his sword. The fire lord drew his fire sword. The blade burst into flames.

Marsonee, followed by the townspeople of Rone, flooded into the town square. Simultaneously, the fire soldiers of Flar rushed through the main gate and began falling into formation behind their demonic leader. Flar's eyes glowed an intense, evil red. He chuckled.

"Is this what you want, boy?" Flar grimaced. "You know that my fire army

81

will butcher these pathetic peasants."

Marsonee stepped forward to the brave knight. "They will fight for you," he whispered.

"I cannot ask the people of Rone to sacrifice their lives for me," the Golden Knight replied.

"These people, poor as they may be, do so willingly for their city and King," Marsonee said. "Just as all of us have done for you on this journey."

"I await your answer, Golden Knight!" Flar shouted out across the courtyard. "Will you lead the lost people of Rone to their ultimate doom?"

The Golden Knight drove his sword into the ground and knelt down on one knee. The townspeople waited. The Golden Knight rose. He pulled his sword out of the dirt and raised the weapon over his head.

"Look," one of the townspeople

called out as he pointed up to the sky.

A ray of bright, pure sunlight penetrated through the dark storm clouds over the city of Rone. Another ray of light followed and then another beam after that. Within moments, thirty or more sun beams of radiant light were shining down on the devastated city.

"What form of treachery is this?" Flar angrily roared. The fire lord shook his flaming sword at the heavens in defiance. He turned and gazed back at the Great Divide crackling in the distance. "You cannot interfere in my realm!"

A white winged stallion covered in sparkling armor galloped through the dark clouds on a beam of sunlight. A young angelic figure, also adorned with battle armor, rode the beautiful creature. The angel's mighty wings powerfully flapped in the wind behind him. He raised his sword over his helmeted head. The stallion reared upward on its hind legs.

"Forward!" the angel ordered. "In the name of your King, I command you forward!"

"Who is it?" the Golden Knight questioned.

"It is Beshtar the archangel," Marsonee replied. "And I promise you,

he did not come alone."

A trumpet sounded followed by another musical blast. The entire sky trembled with the beautiful sound of orchestrated music. The trumpets stopped. The sound of marching feet resonated in the sky. A calvary cohort of hundreds of flying angels darted out from among the clouds. They carried swords and shields. Several of the angels were armed with bows and arrows. One

of the angels landed next to Beshtar.

"Take the catapults in the flank," the archangel ordered. "We cannot have them bothering us in the future."

The angel and his soldiers soared away.

"Infantry division advance!," Beshtar shouted.

Horses, pulling golden chariots, emerged on each of the rays of light. Behind each chariot, rows and rows of angelic soldiers armed with swords and spears marched forward. The townspeople of Rone gazed at the mighty army with confusion and fear.

"It is judgment!" someone called out. "It is judgment for the deeds of our past!"

"Do not fear!" Marsonee assured the crowd. "It is not judgment that you see. It is salvation!"

The angels marched in perfect

unison down the beams of light. As they reached the ground, they spread out in equal columns behind the Golden Knight. Both armies stood facing one another. Beshtar carefully guided his winged horse to gracefully land beside Marsonee. The handsome archangel dismounted.

"My dear friend," Beshtar said. "I had heard that you and your company might be in need of some assistance."

"You have never failed to make a grand appearance," Marsonee replied with a smile.

Outside the city walls, waves of arrows fell down on the fire soldiers guarding the catapults. Angels swooped down from the sky and attacked. After a brief fight, the fire soldiers melted away in panic and ran.

"Your King has violated the laws of the Ancient Book!" Flar growled. "This transgression against the natural order shall not go unpunished!"

"What would you know of the great law?" Beshtar demanded. "All things work for the greater glory of our King."

"Destroy them!" Flar roared.

The fire soldiers rushed forward.

"Attack!" Beshtar commanded as he drew his sword.

The angel army surged forward led by the chariots. The townspeople, led by Marsonee, rushed into the battle with a yell. Angels darted across the sky. The two armies collided in the middle of the town square with a crash of metal and wood. Swords and pitchforks locked in battle. The Golden Knight fought his way toward Flar. The tide of battle slowly began to turn in favor of the angels of Beshtar and the townspeople.

"You shall not escape your justice," the Golden Knight said. "You shall be held accountable for your sins."

"You would dare to challenge me?" Flar retorted. The fire lord extended his black clawed wings. "Then you will fight me in my own element."

Flar rocketed up into the sky.

"Wings," the Golden Knight whispered. Angelic wings materialized on his back in a flash of light. The Golden Knight flew into the air in pursuit of the fire lord.

"Your stupidity knows no bounds," Flar remarked.

"I could say the same for your arrogance," the Golden Knight replied.

The Golden Knight and the evil fire lord exchanged sword blows. They darted and dodged one another's attacks as they flew across the sky. Gradually, they found themselves fighting above the city walls on the outskirts of Rone.

"There is no victory here for you,"

Flar growled. "You have already been tarnished with defeat."

"Hardly," the Golden Knight replied.

Their weapons locked in a fiery explosion. With a quick and skillful parry, the Golden Knight knocked Flar's fire sword from the fire lord's hand. The sword plummeted to the ground below. The flaming blade hit the ground and dug into the dirt. Immediately, the ground began to tremble and quake with a groan. The ground opened and separated into a gapping crack hundreds of feet long. Dirt and rock fell into the crevice as it widened. Flames and smoke erupted out of the dark abyss. Flar laughed in delight.

"What in the Kingdom's name?" the Golden Knight gasped.

"Where is your precious Princess Rainna?" Flar taunted. "Who has protected the Keeper of the Ancient Book from my dark magic? Every moment that you are engaged with me, you lose her."

"If you have harmed her, monster...," the Golden Knight angrily said. He placed the tip of his sword blade against Flar's throat. "...It shall be your end."

"You would strike me down, boy," Flar growled, "even though I am now unarmed? It seems hardly fitting and just for the knight's code that you swear to uphold. You cannot triumph over me. I will always be a part of this world."

The Golden Knight lowered his sword. "It will take time," he said, "but we will change their hearts and lead them back to their King."

"You fool," Flar retorted. "How can you protect them all from me? You are only one. The Great Divide has stood for generations. As long as you remain, I will continue to attack and terrorize the people of this realm."

The Golden Knight clenched his gloved fist. With a mighty blow, he struck Flar's dark helmeted head.

"Away from here, Flar!" the Golden Knight commanded. "Return to the netherworld from whence you came!"

Flar reeled back in shock and pain. The Golden Knight struck the fire lord in his armored chest. Flar plummeted downward toward the flaming abyss. Suddenly, two flaming arms rose out of the fiery crevice and wrapped themselves around Flar's body.

"No!" Flar pleaded as he struggled. "No, I can defeat him!"

A demonic laugh echoed from the underworld.

"I will return for you, Golden Knight!" Flar roared. "I will return to destroy all of you!"

The Golden Knight watched as Flar, the mighty fire lord, was dragged down by the flaming hands and disappeared into the burning darkness. The ground shook violently, and with a cloud of dust, resealed itself. The crack in the earth and Flar were now gone. The Golden Knight slowly descended over the city walls of Rone. He landed in a deserted street. The angelic wings on his back disappeared in a flash of light. In the distance, he could hear the sounds of battle still raging in the city. The Golden Knight started back toward the town square.

Chapter Seven

The Golden Knight returned to the town square fighting his way through Flar's fire soldiers. The army of Beshtar the archangel and the townspeople of Rone were pushing the fire soldiers back. The angelic archers raised their bows. A volley of arrows flew through the air. Rows of fire soldiers fell to the ground. A group of townspeople maneuvered to the left and surprised a division of fire soldiers. A brief struggle ensued before the fire soldiers went running for the main gate. Without their evil leader, the fire army was rapidly losing ground. Beshtar continued to direct the angels with impressive skill. Carefully finding the weak points in the

fire army's formations, Beshtar was able to send his angelic forces to strike at key points creating chaos and confusion within the fire army's ranks.

The Golden Knight saw Marsonee. He was engaged in a sword fight with four of Flar's soldiers. The angel's wing was still slightly smoking from the sword wound that he had received earlier. The Golden Knight fought his way toward him. Marsonee brushed the fire soldiers aside, throwing them through the air with one motion of his hand.

"You are still hurt," the Golden Knight said.

"Yes," Marsonee answered, "but still able to fight."

"The King's army can continue this battle without us," the Golden Knight replied. "We must get to the cathedral and make sure Rainna is safe."

"Agreed," Marsonee said.

They rushed across the town square to Beshtar. Two angels stood beside him.

"Can you hold them?" the Golden Knight asked.

"Hold them?" Beshtar laughed. "We are going to defeat them."

"Of that my friend," Marsonee grinned, "I have no doubt."

The Golden Knight and Marsonee raced toward the church of Rone. Franco carried Rainna's body out the cathedral doors. Demetrius followed him carrying the Ancient Book. Franco slowly descended the steps. Marsonee's eyes widened in shock as the Golden Knight slid to a halt.

"Oh, no," the Golden Knight whispered. There was a flash of light and he was transformed back into Justin. "What happened?"

"We tried to save her," Franco gasped. "We were too late. Murlox had already gotten to her before we arrived."

Franco placed Rainna's lifeless body on the ground. Justin knelt down and cradled her in his arms. Tears welled up in his eyes.

"Is she...?" he asked.

"She is gone, my son," Demetrius answered. "I am so sorry."

"It cannot be right," Justin said. "She was the protector of the Ancient Book."

"Where is the Book now?" Marsonee questioned. "Has it been kept safe from the clutches of Murlox?"

"We have it," Demetrius answered. "It is safe."

Justin wept. He raised his fist toward the heavens. "My life for her life!" Justin called out. "I offer myself in sacrifice for her! Can you not hear me?

Take me and not her!"

Justin closed his eyes in sadness and embraced Rainna's body. Overhead, the dark clouds slowly began to disappear and move away. The sky was clear and blue. The sun was shining. A lone white dove descended from the heavens and landed beside them. Justin opened his eyes. He reached out his hand. The dove pranced over to him. The bird spread its wings and flew away. A rain drop fell from the sky and struck Rainna's face. The tiny drop of water ran down her forehead, across her nose, and touched her lips. More rain began to fall. Soon it was a downpour.

"How?" Franco asked. "There are no clouds."

"The rain will save the city," Demetrius remarked. He turned to look at the burning homes of Rone. "It will extinguish the fires of destruction wrought by the armies of Flar."

Justin remembered the old man that he had helped at the well that he had met just days ago. He reflected on what the old man had told him: Water is life.

"The King does not abandon his faithful," Justin humbly whispered. "If it be thy will..."

Rainna opened her eyes and saw the bright glory of the Kingdom. The skies were blue and clear. There was no Great Divide. Angelic creatures flew overhead and darted across the sky in an effortless motion. The castle walls were a dazzling white and the streets were paved with bricks of gold. The sound of beautiful music played. Rainna rose to her feet and moved forward. She felt as if she had no weight.

"Where am I?" Rainna called out.

"Is this the Kingdom?"

There was an orb of bright light before her. It radiated a warmth that Rainna could not describe. In the center of the light, the King stood in royal glory.

"It is not your time, my dear one," the King said. "Where you are, you were not meant to be."

"I do not wish to leave," Rainna replied.

"Reach out for my hand, precious Rainna, and you will be saved," the King said. He extended his arm out to her.

Rainna hesitated. "Am I the Keeper?"

"Oh, yes," the King answered. "You are the Keeper. And you are so much more."

Rainna reached out and took the King's hand. There was a blinding flash of light followed by darkness.

The Prince appeared before them, transfigured in robes of dazzling white. The rain could not touch the Prince. He remained perfectly dry. Marsonee and Demetrius knelt down on one knee.

"My lord and my prince," they said.

Franco stood paralyzed in amazement. The Prince walked over toward him and gently placed his hand on Franco's cheek. Franco fell to his knees in the mud.

"Your way has been restored to you," the Prince calmly spoke. "Peace be with you. Not the peace of this world do I bestow unto you, but a peace that only I can give to you."

"Will you not save her?" Justin asked. "She was the Keeper of your ancient Word."

"I am the Word made flesh that came into this world ages ago," the Prince replied. "I dwell inside of her as she dwells inside of me. You must keep my words so I shall remain with you and so that you may have life eternal in the glory of your King."

The Prince knelt down and rubbed his hand against Rainna's soaked hair.

"She believed in you," Justin said, water streaming down his face. "We all believe in you."

"Marsonee, my faithful servant," the Prince commanded. The archangel rose to his feet. "Give to me the ring."

Marsonee was momentarily startled. He reached into his jacket pocket. He handed the Prince the simple, gold band.

"I would trade my life for hers," Justin said.

"Your life is her life," the Prince replied. "You are bound together in a circle which can never be broken. This ring, the ring of life, is a symbol of that

circle."

The Prince slid the ring onto Rainna's finger. He placed Justin's hand onto Rainna's hand.

"As the King has sent me to you, I now send you out into this world," the Prince instructed. "All things work in time for the glory of the King."

The Prince stood and raised his arms toward the heavens. He vanished from their view. Suddenly, Rainna gasped for breath and opened her eyes. She softly smiled.

"You are alive," Justin said. He embraced her. "Thank the King, you are alive."

The rain stopped.

Chapter Eight

The battle for Rone had ended. Flar's fire army had been defeated and was in retreat. There was much damage and destruction to the city. Despite the rain that had fallen, many of the buildings and straw homes were still burning and sending large black clouds of smoke into the air. Beshtar had instructed his angel army to help the townspeople battle the fires. Angels darted across the evening sky dropping buckets of water on the rooftops. The townspeople were working together helping those who were hurt and saving what possessions they could from the rubble. Women and small children were being flown to safety. Others had made shelter and were preparing food.

Beshtar and Marsonee stood by the cathedral steps. "You have fulfilled the wishes of your King," Beshtar said. He placed his hand on Marsonee's shoulder. "You are free to return with us to the Kingdom."

"But I am wounded, my friend," Marsonee replied.

"All wounds do heal," Beshtar said. "You have fought bravely, Marsonee. Your skills as a warrior have not diminished. Your place among the mightiest archangels remains."

"Wounds only fade," Marsonee said. "They can never truly heal. Do you know of the wound of which I speak?"

"Yes, of course."

"Then you know it is not my wing."

"Forgiveness can be found in the Kingdom," Beshtar reminded him. "There is nothing more that you owe. Surely you do not believe that

forgiveness can be found in the mortal realm?"

Marsonee glanced over at Justin and Rainna. "Yes," Marsonee said with a slight smile. "I believe there is still much to do and to be found in this world for me. I wish to remain."

"The King shall honor your wishes," Beshtar said. He extended his hand. Marsonee took it. "I shall wait for the time when you return to us, my old friend. May the King always walk with you on your journey."

"As He does with you," Marsonee replied. "Come. Let me properly introduce you to my friends."

"Not this time," Beshtar said. "My place is with the angels. We will finish what needs to be done here and then we shall be gone."

Marsonee walked off alone toward his friends. Justin helped Rainna to her feet.

"I have seen the Kingdom," she said. "I have seen a world where the Great Divide does not exist."

"You need to rest," Justin replied.

"The Book? Is it safe?" she asked.

"Yes, princess," Franco answered. "It is with us."

Demetrius placed the Book in her hands. "I believe this belongs to you."

"It belongs to all of us," Rainna remarked.

"You have won a great victory today," Marsonee said. "You have proven yourself worthy of the Golden Knight."

Justin turned away.

"What troubles you, boy?" Marsonee asked.

"We cannot stay here," Justin answered.

Demetrius nodded and sighed.

"We may have beaten Flar today,"

Justin continued. "We know he will be back. As long as we stay here, we place all of these people in danger."

"What would you have us do?" Rainna questioned. "Where are we to go?"

"We must find the other knights," Justin said. "We must build an army to defeat Flar once and for all. Only then, will the people and this land be free."

"The Book speaks of another kingdom established generations ago following the first great trial of faith by the knights of the Prince," Rainna remarked.

"How do you know that is not some fairy tale someone tells their children at bedtime?" Franco sarcastically asked.

"It is in the Book," Rainna replied. "It must be true."

"There is such a place," Demetrius said. "It is called the Outremer."

"Outremer?" Justin repeated.

"Yes," the old priest replied. "It is from an ancient language which means the land beyond the seas."

"Will you take us there?" Justin said. "Do you know the way?"

"The way will be revealed to you," Demetrius remarked, "just as all things have been revealed, through the wisdom of the Ancient Book. My place is here in Rone. I cannot join you on your quest."

"What can you do here?" Franco asked, looking around. "There is nothing left."

"Ah, my young friend," Demetrius chuckled, gently slapping Franco on the cheek. "There is much these two old hands can do when joined by the hands and hearts of others. We shall rebuild this city, stone by stone, and it shall never burn again. Yes, we shall rebuild this city and it shall have no walls. And for the first time in countless generations, the cathedral of Rone will be opened to share the joy of the King."

The townspeople cheered. Demetrius, his hands raised over his head, skipped off to join them.

"You have to admire that crazy old man's passion," Franco remarked. He kicked at the dirt with his sandals. "I am going to turn myself in for my past crimes. I am a thief. I have a debt to pay."

Justin glanced over to Marsonee. The archangel stepped forward.

"It is said that the Golden Knight will choose the ones who will follow him," Marsonee remarked. "I did not see a thief today. I saw someone who was strong and brave."

"I have chosen you, Franco," Justin said. "Tonight your door will be unlocked. You are free to go if that is

what you want. I ask you to join us."

"Me? A knight?"

"We have found the Keeper in an unlikely place. In several hours, we shall know your fate as well," Marsonee remarked. "But for now, come. Let me prepare my special recipe of wild hog for you."

The early morning came with the crowing of the rooster. Justin and Marsonee had assembled in the chamber of the stone crosses. Candles lined the walls. Justin moved around the room, staring at the stone statues.

"Did you know all of them?" he asked.

"Most," Marsonee replied. "They were fishermen, shepherds, and even a tax collector. Once they heard the calling of their King, they were never the same."

"I hope we are worthy of the

tremendous task before us," Justin said.

"The King does not see us as we are, but rather as He has made us to be," Marsonee answered. "Already I have seen you change."

Rainna entered the room.

"I went to Franco's door," she said. "He was not there."

Justin sighed. "I had thought maybe..."

"We cannot force him to join with us," Marsonee remarked. "We must respect his free will."

Justin raised the cross necklace to his lips. There was a blinding flash of light and the Golden Knight appeared. He raised his helmet visor to reveal Justin's face.

"Rainna, if you will join me at the head table on the right side," the Golden Knight instructed.

"Of course," she answered. Rainna

walked over to the cross table. She placed the Book in the center. The Golden Knight removed the necklace from the sword's handle and placed it around Rainna's neck. She smiled.

Suddenly, Demetrius stormed into the room.

"Wait!" the old priest called out.

The Golden Knight and Rainna turned.

"There is another," Demetrius said.

Franco walked into the chamber dressed in a white robe.

"He wanted to be dressed appropriately for this day," Demetrius finished.

"I ask for forgiveness," Franco humbly said. "I ask to join you."

"Franco, if you will join me at the head table at the left side," the Golden Knight said. Franco did. The Golden Knight removed the cross necklace from the sword's handle and placed it around Franco's neck. "Rainna, remove your boots. Franco, please remove your sandals."

As Rainna and Franco did as they were instructed, Marsonee walked to the corner of the chamber. Demetrius handed him a small bowl filled with water and a cloth. The archangel returned to the head table. He knelt down and washed Rainna's feet.

"I cleanse you and purify you with water," Marsonee chanted, "to sanctify you as a servant to all people, to the Golden Knight, and to your King."

When he had finished, Marsonee washed Franco's feet. Then the archangel rose and walked back to where Demetrius stood. The Golden Knight extended his arms.

"I have chosen you. The King has chosen you. We are the heralds to an age of light," he said. "Remove the swords."

Rainna and Franco simultaneously brought their cross necklaces to their lips. They reached out to the swords. The Book rose and hovered above the stone cross. There was a blinding flash of pure white light. Rainna stood transformed in a suit of silver armor. She held the sword above her head. Her helmet was open to show her face. Her cape flowed behind her. Franco was clothed in bronze armor. He too held the sword above his head. His armor resembled more of the style of the Golden Knight.

"It is awesome," Franco whispered. He flipped open his helmet visor to show his face. "It is true."

"You are the Silver Knight, Rainna, the Keeper of the Ancient Book," the Golden Knight said. "We are joined as no other two knights ever shall be."

The Silver Knight lowered her

sword. She placed it in her sheath and took the Book in her hands.

"You are the Bronze Knight, Franco, a mighty warrior who shall know no equal in battle," the Golden Knight continued. "Henceforth, you will be known at this table as Francis."

The Bronze Knight placed his sword on the cross table and lowered himself to one knee. He prayed silently for a moment before rising back to his feet.

"Where do we go now?" the Bronze Knight asked. "Do we search for Outremer?"

"Yes," the Golden Knight replied. He turned to the Silver Knight "We go to the coastal territories where we can find passage. But first, we shall free your father and mother from Flar's dungeon."

"Let the adventure begin then," Marsonee said. He drew his sword and raised it. The three knights did the same with their weapons.

"For the King!" they called out. "For the King!"

The afternoon came to Rone. There was still much activity among the townspeople. Justin watched as the people walked up the cathedral's steps and entered the old church. He smiled. Justin mounted his horse. Rainna, Franco, and Marsonee rode up beside him.

"Are you ready, boy?" Marsonee asked.

"We will return," Justin answered. "We will save this land."

"Of course, we will," Franco confidently replied.

They rode out of the city and headed toward the coast.

About the Authors

Justin Clark is a student at Cass High School and a member of its Art Club. Justin loves anime, fantasy and superheroes. He draws and creates many of his own characters including those characters found in The Golden Knight.

His father, Steven Clark, has written stories, songs, stage plays and poems since high school. He is a graduate of Kennesaw State University with a degree in history. The Clark family (Steven, Leslie, Justin, Jason and Brooke) live in Cartersville, Georgia.

About the Illustrator

Alison Fuller is the illustrator for The Golden Knight #3: Rainna Falls.

Alison Fuller has grown up all over Georgia and has been drawing ever since she asked her mom for a piece of scrap paper in church one day. Alison can be found doing art for birthday parties or selling her originals at conventions. This was her first time illustrating for a book and she was super excited to be a part of The Golden Knight series. She'd like to thank her family and friends for the encouraging words while working on this project and she hopes you enjoyed the book! She is a graduate of Unity Christian School. Alison lives in Rome, Georgia with her family and her cat who likes to help out by sitting on her art supplies.

The Adventure Awaits!

Like Us on Facebook!

www.facebook.com/TheGoldenKnightSeries

The Golden Knight #1
The Boy is Summoned

In the beginning, the Kingdom was ruled by a wise and just King who ruled by the laws written in the ancient Book. The people were protected by the archangels and the heroic knights. All lived in peace and prospered. Those days are gone...

Flar, the evil fire lord, and his sorceror, Murlox, have banished the King and his angels behind an energy field known as the Great Divide. The Book has been taken. The angels have fallen. The knights are gone. The people suffer. All that remains is the prophecy and a promise of hope.

Join Marsonee the archangel and Princess Rainna as they embark on a journey to bring an innocent farm boy toward his true destiny.

The Golden Knight #2
The Battle For Rone

A legend reborn... Princess Rainna has escaped Devon Castle with the ancient Book of Wisdom. Marsonee the archangel and Justin the farm boy journey to the fallen city of Rone. As their paths collide on a dark road, an even greater challenge awaits them in the catacombs of the old cathedral of Rone. Can Justin remove the sword and become the Golden Knight? Is the Keeper among us? Who is the mysterious figure known only as the Prince?

Flar, the evil fire lord, and his sorcerer, Murlox, have learned the identity of the Keeper and are determined to prevent the prophecy from being fulfilled. Summoning a powerful Demon from the pits of the underworld, Flar and Murlox lead an army of fire soldiers to attack Rone. New allies and new dangers await our heroes as the Keeper is revealed, the Golden Knight is reborn and the battle for the ancient city of Rone begins.

CPSIA information can be obtained
at www.ICGtesting.com
Printed in the USA
FFOW03n1137010814
6581FF